187214

PowerKids Readers:
The Bilingual Library of the
United States of America™

DELAWARE

VANESSA BROWN

Traducción al español: María Cristina Brusca

The Rosen Publishing Group's
PowerKids Press™ & **Editorial Buenas Letras**™
New York

Published in 2005 by The Rosen Publishing Group, Inc.
29 East 21st Street, New York, NY 10010

First Edition

Photo Credits: Cover © Gene Ahrens/SuperStock, Inc.; p. 5 © Joe Sohm/The Image Works; p. 7 © 2002 Geoatlas; pp. 9, 21, 23, 31 (Industry) © Kevin Fleming/Corbis; pp. 11, 31 (settlers) © Stock Montage/SuperStock, Inc.; p. 13 © Bettmann/Corbis; pp. 17, 31 (Pierre Samuel du Pont, Canby) © Time Life Pictures/Getty Images; p. 19 © Bob Krist/Corbis; pp. 25, 30 (Capital) © David Forbert/SuperStock, Inc.; pp. 26, 30 (Peach Blossom) © Gary Holscher/Getty Images; p. 30 (Blue Hen Chicken) © Robert Dowling/Corbis; p. 30 (American Holly) © Sally A. Morgan; Ecoscene/Corbis; p. 31 (Cary) National Archives of Canada C-029977; p. 31 (Bayard) © Corbis; p. 31 (Nathans) © Getty Images; p. 31 (Pete du Pont) © Shepard Sherbell/Corbis Saba; p. 31 (Constitution) NARA

Library of Congress Cataloging-in-Publication Data

Brown, Vanessa, 1963–
Delaware / Vanessa Brown ; traducción al español, María Cristina Brusca. — 1st ed.
p. cm. — (The bilingual library of the United States of America) Includes bibliographical references and index. ISBN 1-4042-3073-4 (library binding)
1. Delaware — Juvenile literature. I. Title. II. Series.

F164.3.B765 2005
975.1–dc22

2005001246

Manufactured in the United States of America

Due to the changing nature of Internet links, Editorial Buenas Letras has developed an online list of Web sites related to the subject of this book. This site is updated regularly. Please use this link to access the list:

http://www.buenasletraslinks.com/ls/delaware

Contents

Contenido

Welcome to Delaware

Delaware is known as the First State. Delaware was the first state to agree with the U.S. Constitution. The date on the flag marks that day, December 7, 1787.

Bienvenidos a Delaware

Delaware es conocido como el Primer Estado. Delaware fue el primer estado en ratificar la Constitución de E.U.A., el 7 de diciembre de 1787. En la bandera aparece esa fecha.

DECEMBER 7, 1787

Delaware Flag and State Seal

Bandera y escudo de Delaware

Delaware Geography

Delaware borders Pennsylvania, Maryland, and New Jersey. Delaware's eastern border runs along the Delaware River and the Atlantic Ocean.

Geografía de Delaware

Delaware linda con los estados de Pensilvania, Maryland y Nueva Jersey. El río Delaware y el océano Atlántico forman la frontera este de Delaware.

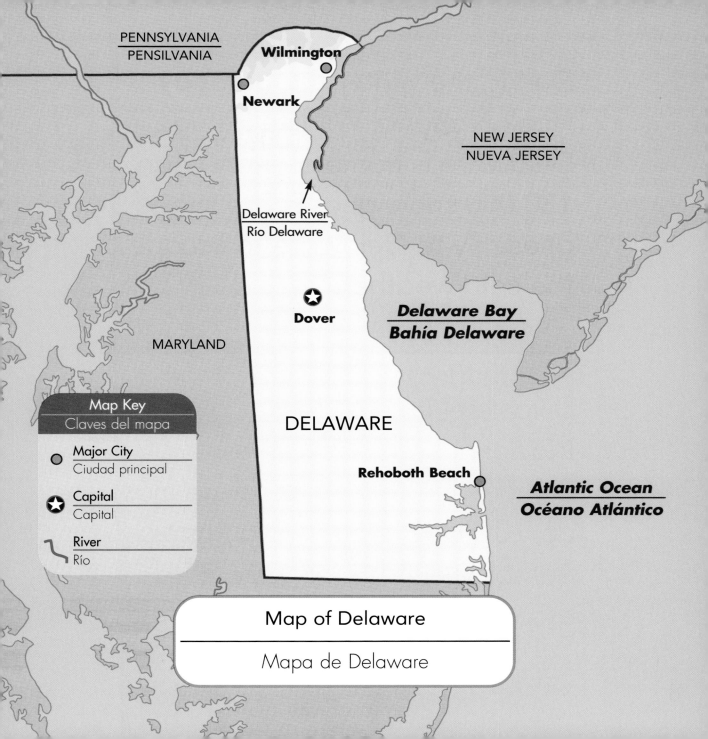

PENNSYLVANIA
PENSILVANIA

Wilmington

Newark

NEW JERSEY
NUEVA JERSEY

Delaware River
Río Delaware

MARYLAND

★ **Dover**

Delaware Bay
Bahía Delaware

DELAWARE

Rehoboth Beach

Atlantic Ocean
Océano Atlántico

Map Key
Claves del mapa

Major City
Ciudad principal

★ Capital
Capital

River
Río

Map of Delaware

Mapa de Delaware

During the winter the Bombay Hook National Wildlife Refuge in Delaware is home of more than 130,000 snow geese. The snow geese fly to Delaware to escape the cold weather.

Durante el invierno, el Refugio Nacional de la Vida Silvestre Bombay Hook es el hogar de más de 130,000 gansos nival. Estos gansos vuelan a Delaware para escapar del clima frío.

Snow Geese Flock in the Water

Una bandada de gansos nival en el agua

Delaware History

Swedish and Dutch settlers were the first Europeans to arrive in Delaware. In 1682, the state became an English colony.

Historia de Delaware

Los colonos suecos y holandeses fueron los primeros europeos en llegar a Delaware. En 1682, el estado comenzó a ser una colonia inglesa.

Peter Stuyvesant, Dutch Colonial Governor

Peter Stuyvesant, gobernador holandés de la colonia

On July 4, 1776, Delaware and the rest of the English colonies signed the Declaration of Independence. With this the colonies became the United States of America.

El 4 de julio de 1776, Delaware y el resto de las colonias inglesas firmaron la Declaración de Independencia. Por este acto las colonias se convirtieron en los Estados Unidos de América.

The Signing of the Declaration of Independence

Firma de la Declaración de Independencia

Caesar Rodney rode his horse all night from Pennsylvania to vote in favor of independence. Rodney's vote helped Delaware win its independence.

Caesar Rodney cabalgó toda la noche desde Filadelfia para votar a favor de la independencia. El voto de Rodney ayudó a Delaware a ganar su independencia.

Quarter Showing Rodney's Historical Ride

Moneda de la cabalgata histórica de Rodney

The du Pont family has lived in Delaware since the 1800s. The du Ponts have been important inventors, businessmen, and goverment officials in Delaware. Pierre-Samuel du Pont worked to make Delaware schools better.

La familia du Pont ha vivido en Delaware desde los comienzos de 1800. Los du Pont han sido importantes inventores, empresarios y funcionarios del gobierno de Delaware. Pierre-Samuel du Pont trabajó para mejorar las escuelas de Delaware.

FIFTEEN CENTS

JANUARY 31, 1927

TIME

The Weekly Newsmagazine

Pierre du Pont on a 1927 Cover of *Time* Magazine

Pierre du Pont en la tapa de la revista Time, en 1927

Living in Delaware

Many people in Delaware enjoy fishing. Delawareans catch saltwater fish in Delaware Bay and the Atlantic Ocean.

La vida en Delaware

Mucha gente en Delaware disfruta de la pesca. En la bahía Delaware y en el océano Atlántico, los delawareños pescan peces de agua salada.

Fly-fishing on the Delaware River

Pesca con mosca en el río Delaware

Delaware has a long coast with sunny beaches. Millions of visitors enjoy Delaware's beaches every year.

Delaware tiene una larga costa de playas soleadas. Cada año, millones de visitantes disfrutan de las playas de Delaware.

Visitors Enjoying the Beach in Delaware

Turistas disfrutando de la playa en Delaware

Delaware Today

Delaware is home to many banks and businesses. The DuPont company is the largest employer in Delaware.

Delaware, hoy

Las oficinas centrales de muchos bancos y empresas se encuentran en Delaware. La companía Dupont es el principal empleador de Delaware.

A View of Downtown Wilmington, Delaware

Una vista del centro de Wilmington, Delaware

Wilmington, Newark, and Rehoboth Beach are important cities in Delaware. Dover is the capital of Delaware.

Wilmington, Newark y Rehoboth Beach son ciudades importantes de Delaware. Dover es la capital de Delaware.

Old State House in Dover

Antigua casa de gobierno en Dover

Activity:
Let's Draw Delaware's State Flower

The peach blossom became Delaware's state flower in 1895.

Actividad:
Dibujemos la flor del estado de Delaware

La flor del durazno es la flor del estado de Delaware desde 1895.

1

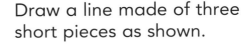

Draw a line made of three short pieces as shown.

Dibuja una línea formada por tres trazos cortos.

2

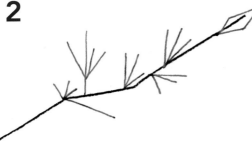

On each of the pieces, add groups of short lines. Draw a diamond shape at the right end of the line.

A cada uno de los trazos agrégale grupos de trazos más cortos. Dibuja la forma de un diamante en el lado derecho de la línea.

3

Make leaves using the short lines from step 2.

Dibuja hojas utilizando las líneas cortas del paso 2.

4

Double the main line to make the stem of the flower. For the flowers draw three circles and four curved lines connected to a single point. From the center circles, draw a few lines and dots at their end.

Traza líneas dobles para dibujar la rama principal. Para dibujar la flor traza tres círculos y cuatro líneas curvas que se junten en un solo punto. A partir del círculo central dibuja varias líneas con puntos en sus extremos.

Timeline

Cronología

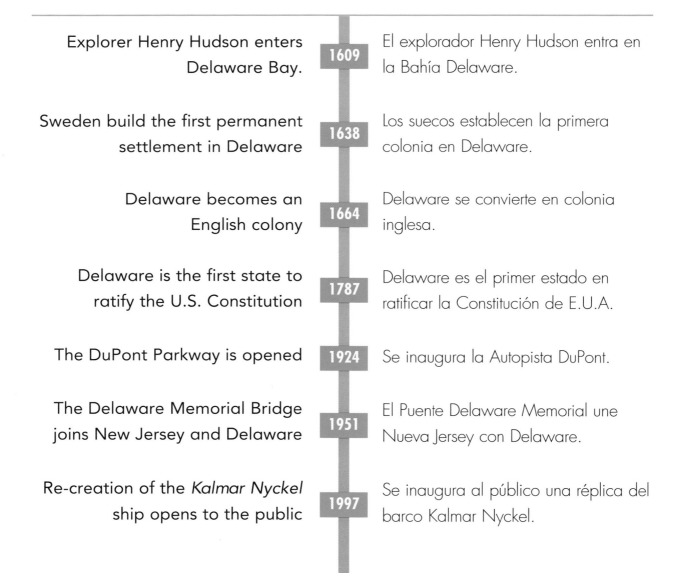

Explorer Henry Hudson enters Delaware Bay.	**1609**	El explorador Henry Hudson entra en la Bahía Delaware.
Sweden build the first permanent settlement in Delaware	**1638**	Los suecos establecen la primera colonia en Delaware.
Delaware becomes an English colony	**1664**	Delaware se convierte en colonia inglesa.
Delaware is the first state to ratify the U.S. Constitution	**1787**	Delaware es el primer estado en ratificar la Constitución de E.U.A.
The DuPont Parkway is opened	**1924**	Se inaugura la Autopista DuPont.
The Delaware Memorial Bridge joins New Jersey and Delaware	**1951**	El Puente Delaware Memorial une Nueva Jersey con Delaware.
Re-creation of the *Kalmar Nyckel* ship opens to the public	**1997**	Se inaugura al público una réplica del barco Kalmar Nyckel.

Delaware Events

March
Delaware Kite Festival at Cape Henlopen State Park in Lewes

April
Irish Festival at Hagley Museum near Wilmington

May
Old Dover Days
Winterthur Point to Point Horse Race
Tour du Pont Bicycle Race

June
Miller 500 Stock Car Race in Dover

July
Delaware State Fair in Harrington

September
Nanticoke Indian Pow Wow near Oak Orchard
MBNA 400 stock car race in Dover

December
Candlelight tours of historic homes in Newcastle

Eventos en Delaware

Marzo
Festival Delaware de la cometa, en el Parque Estatal Cabo Henlopen, en Lewes

Abril
Festival irlandés en el Museo Hagley cerca de Wilmington

Mayo
Días del antiguo Dover
Carrera de caballos de punto a punto de Winterthur
Carrera de bicicletas Tour du Pont

Junio
Carrera de automóviles Miller 500 Stock

Julio
Feria estatal de Delaware, en Harrington

Septiembre
Pow Wow de la tribu Nanticoke, cerca de Oak Orchard
Carrera de automóviles MBNA 400, en Dover

Diciembre
Gira de casas históricas a la luz de las velas, en Newcastle

Delaware Facts/Datos sobre Delaware

<u>Population</u>
783,000

<u>Población</u>
783,000

<u>Capital</u>
Dover

<u>Capital</u>
Dover

<u>State Motto</u>
Liberty and
Independence

<u>Lema del estado</u>
Libertad e
Independencia

<u>State Flower</u>
Peach Blossom

<u>Flor del estado</u>
Flor del durazno

<u>State Bird</u>
Blue Hen Chicken

<u>Ave del estado</u>
Gallina azul

<u>State Nickname</u>
The First State

<u>Mote del estado</u>
Primer Estado

<u>State Tree</u>
American Holly

<u>Árbol del estado</u>
Acebo americano

<u>State Song</u>
"Our Delaware"

<u>Canción del estado</u>
"Nuestro Delaware"

Famous Delawareans/Delawareños famosos

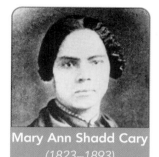
Mary Ann Shadd Cary *(1823–1893)*
Newspaper editor
Editora de periódico

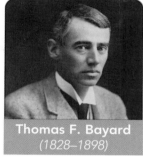
Thomas F. Bayard *(1828–1898)*
U.S. Senator
Senador de E.U.A.

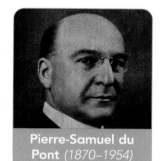
Pierre-Samuel du Pont *(1870–1954)*
Businessman
Empresario

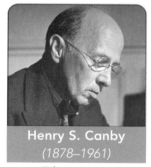
Henry S. Canby *(1878–1961)*
Editor, writer
Editor y escritor

Daniel Nathans *(1928–1999)*
Physician
Médico

Pete du Pont *(1935–)*
Delaware governor
Gobernador de Delaware

Words to Know/Palabras que debes saber

border
frontera

industry
industria

settlers
colonos

U.S. Constitution
Constitución de
E.U.A.

31

Here are more books to read about Delaware:
Otros libros que puedes leer sobre Delaware:

In English/En inglés:

Delaware
America the Beautiful
by Blashfield, Jean F.
Children's Press, 2000

Delaware
From Sea to Shining Sea
by Miller, Amy
Children's Press, 2002

Words in English: 248   Palabras en español: 284

Index

Índice